White Deer

GHOSTS OF THE FOREST

White Deer
GHOSTS OF THE FOREST

PHOTOGRAPHS BY
Jeff Richter

TEXT BY
John Bates

Nature's Press
MERCER, WISCONSIN

Copyright © 2007 Jeff Richter; Text © 2007 John Bates except
Ojibwe Story, Preface and Photographers Introduction; Ojibwe Story
of the White Deer © Ernie St. Germain.
All rights reserved. No use or copying of any of the content of this
book is lawful without permission of the publisher.
Published by Nature's Press, Jeff and Rosy Richter
PO Box 371, Mercer, WI 54547. Phone 715-476-2938.

Softcover ISBN-13: 978-0-9741883-1-7
Hardcover ISBN-13: 978-0-9741883-2-4

All images contained in this book were shot on film. No computer
manipulation or alteration of the images has been used.
Design by Patricia Bickner, A New Leaf, www.anewleaf-books.com
Printed in USA; Menomonee Falls, Wisconsin

Contents

For Rosy, my nature girl.

For Mom & Dad, who always encouraged us.

*For all the talented people who helped
make this book a reality.*

"DESPITE THE GROWING TREND IN DIGITAL PHOTOGRAPHY, JEFF'S
PURIST APPROACH OF USING RAW COLOR AND LIGHT, AND UNCANNY
ABILITY TO CAPTURE PROFOUND BEAUTY IN THAT 'PRECISE WILD
MOMENT,' ARE TESTAMENT TO HIS DEDICATION TO PRESERVING ALL
THAT IS NATURAL."

—TESS GALLUN

Preface

IT'S IMPORTANT TO ME TO BE CLEAR ABOUT THE PHOTOGRAPHIC METHODS THAT I USE IN THE IMAGES PRESENTED IN THIS BOOK.

All of the images contained in this book were shot on film (mostly slide film) and every effort was made to stay true to the original.

Modern day photography, to my dismay, seems to have detoured into a never-ending discussion of computers, pixels and Photoshop. The technological changes absorbed by the photo industry over the last 10 years have been off the charts compared with what transpired in the previous century. Obviously and unquestionably, there are some advantages with the new digital "film" being shot by more and more photographers. However, with the incredible power of the computer to alter and manipulate comes added responsibility on the part of the photographer to be honest about what they present to the public.

Increasingly, in my opinion, natural scenes being depicted in galleries, art shows and publications are crossing the line of believability. I know my customers, the general public, and I myself expect a level of authenticity when viewing nature photography. The computer has largely turned the realism of photography on its head—and in the process has thrown a cloud of skepticism over the heads of all photographers, mainly because of a growing segment of manipulated work being marketed as real.

The constant assertion by digital shooters that what they do is no different from what photographers of the past did with filters and darkroom techniques does not hold up to any objective measure, in my mind.

Don't get me wrong. I'm not against all digital

I'M STILL SHOOTING FILM, AND I HAVE NO PLANS TO SWITCH ANY TIME SOON.

shooting. There are plenty of shooters that use it in an ethical way and it's here to stay. It's just not for me. Not once when I've been in the field, surrounded by unending natural beauty, have I thought, "Man, I can't wait to get home and fix, enhance, manipulate this incredible scene in front of me."

Being a professional nature photographer has enriched my life in unimaginable ways. Yet for every memorable image there's a garbage can full of shots I worked just as hard for. Particularly when working with wildlife, I'm fond of using the adage, "What can go wrong, will go wrong." It's uncanny how after waiting for hours, perhaps days, for just the right moment, something will happen to make it vanish right before your eyes. Whether it's the only cloud in the sky all day blocking the light you need, a scolding blue jay exposing your presence, or a simple camera malfunction ruining your efforts at a critical moment, much of what happens is out of our control. However, with that uncertainty comes a lot of excitement when you're able to record a moment that's both unexpected and wonderful. Early on, you find that patience and perseverance play as large a role as equipment and skill in returning with marketable images.

Increasingly, present-day photography is becoming less about photographic skills and time in the woods and more about computer skills.

In days past, good photographers were the ones that produced memorable images despite the limitations of film and camera and the frequent lack of cooperation from their subjects. In days past, a photograph was a moment in time which the viewer assumed was rooted in reality. The computer has significantly blurred those truths.

The bottom line is, I remain unconvinced about all the hype surrounding digital technology. As of this writing, I've personally never been on a computer, I'm still shooting film, and I have no plans to switch anytime soon. I'll continue to endeavor to stay true to nature.

—Jeff Richter

I found many examples of how white deer affected people's lives during my searches for the elusive albino. Several communities displayed stuffed albino deer which had frquented their area. Whether they were hit by a car or illegally shot, people wanted to preserve the memory of seeing these unique creatures.

Photographer's Introduction

ONCE, MANY MOONS PAST, IN THE DEEP WOODS OF THE NORTH, THERE EXISTED A STRANGE AND WONDERFUL CREATURE THAT PASSED GHOST-LIKE THROUGH THE CONSCIOUSNESS OF ALL WHO OBSERVED IT.

A mystical beast that has survived from the time of feather-and-ink journal entries to present-day internet life. An animal so unique and mysterious that it holds a spell over anyone lucky enough to behold its gaze. An animal that to this day has eluded serious scrutiny. I speak of the White Deer.

Even now, after hundreds of sightings over a period of many years, any time I see white deer I feel like I'm entering a modern-day legend. They are so visually unusual and even unsettling that it's hard to ever take them casually. One harkens back to the days spoken of by our native forefathers, early voyageurs, and to still, full-moon nights filled with the drama of survival. Perhaps my attempt to record on film—in essence, to shed some light on these oddities of nature—will only leave deeper secrets.

The fateful day for me occurred about ten years ago here in northern Wisconsin when exploring an area that reportedly has white deer. I came upon a small opening in the woods that any deer hunter would recognize as potentially attractive to feeding deer. It was full of waist-high ferns and my eye was instantly drawn to a stark, white object in its midst. What was at first glance unrecognizable turned instantly to an unforgettable encounter with my first white deer when it raised its head and looked directly at me. I've spent my life traversing field and forest with countless unique wildlife observations, but few have compared with the startled realization of that first white deer. A *Bambi in Wonderland*

moment. I was fascinated—and hooked—on the spot.

Ensuing years have seen me spend well over a hundred days, driving thousands of miles and shooting countless rolls of film searching for and recording these ghosts of the woods. I've either witnessed or had reports of white deer throughout northern Wisconsin, the Upper Peninsula of Michigan and into Minnesota. My best guess is that this area may hold as many as a few hundred; however, that's just an estimate, since to my knowledge none of the states track their populations. Their ranges are obviously somewhat fluid as with any wild populations. However, I suspect there are conditions that exist in certain areas that enable the genetics to remain more viable.

One of those areas happens to be in my back yard of Wisconsin, namely the regions Three Lakes to St. Germain on the south to Presque Isle in the north, Manitowish Waters on the west to Land O' Lakes on the east. Most of Vilas County, really, has for a lot of years been home to white deer. There's some evidence suggesting they may have been present over 150 years ago near Boulder Junction. It's likely, statistics being what they are, that other areas might harbor similar stories. Author John Bates and I were really surprised by how little information of any kind was available about these animals.

My experiences with white deer have been many and varied, both geographically and in regard to individual deer. All have been wild and unrestrained in any way. Behavior was always fascinating and, like all wild animals, unpredictable in terms of their reactions to my presence. At times, a certain individual would tolerate me for some hours, but I could come back the following day and it would disappear at the blink of an eye. A few were so habituated that I saw people hand-feed them, while others were as skittish as a trophy buck, but most

WHENEVER I TALK WITH PEOPLE ABOUT WHITE DEER, ALMOST WITHOUT EXCEPTION THEY RECALL WITH GREAT CLARITY THEIR FIRST SIGHTING.

fell into a middle ground—wary but approachable.

Because of their protected status in some states and the abundance of backyard feeders, many exhibited a tolerance of humans not evident in their hunted brethren.

Other than that tolerance, nothing they did exhibited any peculiar behavior that differentiated them from normal brown deer. Their interactions with other deer ran the gamut of submissiveness to dominance and they appeared to be accepted by brown deer, although I normally saw them in small groups of just a few to perhaps a half dozen. As nearly as I could tell, they were deer in every way.

Up to this point I've been referring to the deer simply as white deer, not albino deer. My belief, over the years, was that I was seeing true albinos, not simply white-colored deer. John Bates and I have had an ongoing difference of opinion about this question for some time. John maintained that true albinos had to have pink eyes. I argued the white velvet, pink noses, cream-colored hooves and unusually-colored eyes indicated they were albinos. Lo and behold, after much searching, John located a researcher and expert in albinism that pretty much confirmed, short of genetic testing, that they do indeed appear to be albinos. John will explain this phenomenon in greater detail later in the book. It really didn't matter to me, photographically speaking. But with John being the smart, scientific type that likes to actually know what he's talking about (so annoying), it was good to finally find vindication in this friendly debate.

I find it interesting that I've seen brown does with both brown and albino fawns, as well as albino does with both brown and albino fawns. I've seen albino bucks with white velvet covering what turned out to be normal-colored antlers when the velvet rubbed off. Most surprising was the light cream cast on the newborn fawns

I found. They exhibited spotting like normal fawns but would gradually lose the spots along with the cream coloration as they matured and evolved into completely white adults.

While the eyes of the albinos were markedly different from normal deer, I never saw one with pink eyes. Mostly they reminded me of a goat's eyes with a light greenish outer area (iris) and a darker center (pupil). Albinos are known to have problems with diminished eyesight. Obviously I didn't have any way to measure visual impairment in the deer by casual observation, but none exhibited any problems making their way through the forest or spotting potential intruders.

Whenever I talk with people about white deer, almost without exception they recall with great clarity their first sighting. Rarely have I encountered a species that has delighted and astonished the senses of all who've been in the presence of these unique creatures. Many are the unforgettable moments I've shared with them, ranging from comical to spiritual. Memories of a momentary glimpse of one, seemingly floating through a foggy forest bathed in twilight, has left me changed. Are these white deer nothing more than genetic freaks of nature that deserve nothing more than to be dismissed as oddballs; or like the white buffalo, an animal that causes us to think about the natural world and our place in it in a different context. I know my life has been enriched in ways only nature can, touched to the core, by the white deer, ghost deer, spirit deer.

Even now, after hundreds of sightings over a period of many years, any time I see white deer I feel like I'm entering a modern-day legend. They are so visually unusual and even unsettling that it's hard to ever take them casually.

This image was taken in almost the exact spot at Dairyman's Resort in Boulder Junction as the photo that appeared in *Life Magazine* in 1950.

Magic

BY JOHN BATES

MY WIFE MARY AND I FIRST SAW AN
ALBINO DEER JUST AT THAT MOMENT
WHEN DARK HAD SHOULDERED DAY FROM
THE LANDSCAPE.

We were surveying singing frogs for the Wisconsin DNR
and had our minds tuned to all things amphibious, when
our headlights swept around a corner and onto a white doe
standing on the edge of the woods. The doe gave us one look,
turned, leapt back into the woods, and was gone—a phantom
observation of a phantom deer.

Mary and I were stunned at first, but then the superlatives
rolled. We may as well have seen a UFO for all the excitement
it generated, and all from an animal we've seen literally thousands of times. An animal, in fact, so overpopulated in our
forests that I've argued for years how we need to dramatically
reduce their number.

But we'd never seen an albino deer.

Interestingly, we've seen many albino birds, and while
they've been a curiosity, they've never drawn the exclamations
we lavished on this white deer. What was it that made it so
remarkable?

I'm not sure—but for one, it evoked mystery. Einstein, a
man fully cemented in mathematics and science, gave mystery its proper due, writing, "The most beautiful thing we can
experience is the mysterious. It is the source of all true art and
science." Seeing the albino deer created a cascade of questions
that couldn't be answered. Why was it here? Where did it come
from? Was it a breeding doe, and were there white fawns, too?
There was no one to ask, and no way to know.

The deer was beautiful, too. I don't know what peculiar
quality the color white exudes that seems to elicit such a sense
of beauty, but it does. Beauty, it can be argued, is what draws
most of us to the Northwoods. John Muir understood the
importance of beauty to the soul, and wrote: "People need

beauty as well as bread." Bread satisfies, beauty inspires.

Maybe we admired the white deer because of something to do with our childhood and all the fairy tales we were read that were filled with white knights and white dragons. Emerson wrote, "The sun illuminates only the eye of the man, but shines into the eye and the heart of the child. The lover of nature is he … who has retained the spirit of infancy even into the era of manhood." There is a magic in albino animals which is inexplicable. A foolish notion I'm sure, culturally incorrect, plain silly, but there it is—magic. It was magic to see that white deer.

I know the science of recessive genes, adaptation, evolution, and the necessary fitness of the herd. But what does all that matter in the face of magic and beauty? Aldo Leopold, the soul of so much of our ecological understanding and compassion, once buried himself in the muck of a muskrat house to observe the real goings-on in a wetland. He said of the experience, "A hen redhead cruised by with her convoy of ducklings … A Virginia rail nearly brushed my nose. The shadow of a pelican sailed over a pool in which a yellow-leg alighted with warbling whistle: it occurred to me that whereas I write a poem by dint of mighty celebration, the yellow-leg walks a better one just by lifting his foot."

Maybe that's what Mary and I experienced when we saw the white deer—we saw a poem, felt a celebration of this amazing world. Such feelings are not to be analyzed scientifically into their dust and atoms, but left to their initial astonishment, an emotion charged with wonder and appreciation, and one too often forgotten in living our ordinary lives. The deer astonished us, and maybe that's all that needs to be said.

The web of life spins interconnectedness that touches us all. Too often in our busy, artifically-controlled 70° lives we fail to recognise our link to the natural world.

The Genetics — How Many Variations on White Can There Be?

UNDERSTANDING THE GENETICS OF WHITE DEER WOULD CERTAINLY BE EASIER IF ALL WHITE DEER WERE SIMPLY ALBINOS.

But the natural world has had millions of years to evolve variations on every theme, and so not all white deer are true albinos, nor are all albino deer pure white. The color white turns out to be much more complex than "the absence of color" as we were taught in art class.

Over 300 species of North American birds and animals, from whales to snails, have been recorded as having some form of albinism or its many variants. In humans, about one in 20,000 people have one type or another of albinism. Mammalogists estimate that one in 10,000 wild mammal births results in a true albino. In birds, one study of 30,000 wild birds captured in mist nets in Southern California found only 17 displaying some degree of albinism, or one in 1,764 birds. And where the sun can't penetrate and color thus loses its meaning, albinism is actually the normal condition for many fish and invertebrates that live in caves or at great depths in the oceans.

The coloration story of any animal mostly has to do with the presence or absence of melanin, an organic pigment that produces most of the color seen in mammals. Melanin comes in two color ranges: a brownish-black called eumelanin, and a reddish-

tan-yellow called pheomelanin. These two kinds of melanin are blended uniquely in every species of animal to provide essential survival mechanisms, such as absorbing ultraviolet light from the sun so that skin isn't damaged or creating cryptic coloration for camouflage. Dark and light melanins may work alone or in combination to make either plain or multicolored coats, or even multicolored individual hairs.

If you look at your own skin, you'll likely find some areas that appear darker than others because of different amounts of melanin they contain. Most people have more melanin, and thus darker skin, on the backs of their hands and on their faces, while they have less melanin, and thus lighter skin, on the inside of their upper arms. When we tan from exposure to the sun, we are temporarily producing more melanin in those areas of the skin.

Other less important pigments than melanin also produce color, so coloration involves far more complexity than just how much melanin an animal produces.

To the non-scientist, though, too much complexity can be blinding. Instead, most of us just want to be blinded by the beauty of these extraordinary animals. So, let's keep the science as simple as possible by generally describing the many variations on white.

ALBINISM

Albino animals possess all the normal characteristics of their species, but their cells can't produce melanin. Without melanin, an animal, or parts of that animal, typically appear white or pink, or present a bleached look.

THE COLORATION STORY OF ANY ANIMAL MOSTLY HAS TO
DO WITH THE PRESENCE OR ABSENCE OF MELANIN, AN
ORGANIC PIGMENT THAT PRODUCES MOST OF THE COLOR
SEEN IN MAMMALS.

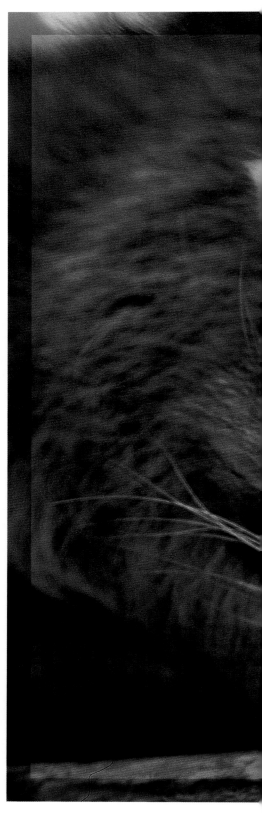

The true test for albinism has always been considered
to be whether an animal has pink irises. Without the
brown-black or red-yellow pigments of melanin coloring
the iris, the eyes of an albino usually appear pink,
because blood vessels behind the lenses show through the
unpigmented irises. But some albinos may show some
color, often light blue or gray, in the irises of their eyes.

An animal can be a pure albino or a partial albino. The
most critical factor in producing melanin is the presence

of a special enzyme called *tyrosinase* – the "TYR" gene. If the TYR gene fails completely, an all-white, light-eyed albino animal will be born. However, the TYR gene can be altered in dozens of ways, producing other albino variations, such as albinos with light eyes but with some color on their fur.

The TYR gene isn't the only player in the melanin game either; other hormones and proteins also impact melanin production, and their presence is determined by additional special genes. In house mice, for instance, a total of 130 genes are known to affect coat color, so for a layman to determine visually whether an animal is albino or not can be very difficult.

LEUCISM

Leucistic animals are white animals that may have some additional pigmentation, and whose eyes are normal in color and function. Leucism produces apparently anomalous white animals from parents that are normally colored. The ratio of white to normal-colored skin can vary considerably between generations, and even between members of the same litter.

Some animals have a leucistic phase for camouflage, such as the snowshoe hare during the winter, while white animals like polar bears are also considered leucistic.

If a white deer has normal-colored eyes, it is very likely leucistic.

AT THE OTHER END OF THE COLOR SPECTRUM, MELANISM
APPEARS WHEN TOO MUCH MELANIN IS PRODUCED, USUALLY
RESULTING IN A VERY DARK SKIN AND PELAGE.

MELANISM

At the other end of the color spectrum, melanism appears when too much melanin is produced, usually resulting in a very dark skin and pelage. In a melanistic deer, the characteristic white areas, like the white throat patch, muzzle band, and inside ears, turn brown or even black.

Melanism rarely appears in deer, but one area in central Texas reports an average of nearly 6 percent melanistic deer, an exceptionally high number. Pelage shades there vary from seal brown to iron gray to blackish-slate.

PIEBALDISM

Piebaldism develops when albinism only affects certain areas of the skin, producing a "pied" or "piebald" effect with irregular patches of white. In piebald individuals, at least some of the cells can produce pigment. The unpigmented patches are due to localized mutations in skin cells that occurred during embryo development. 🦌

Recessive and Dominant Genes

OR WHY SO FEW OF US LIKE MATH

Because albinism is a recessive genetic trait, both parents must carry the recessive gene before an albino fawn can potentially be produced.

All genes are paired in the offspring, one gene in each pair coming from each parent. So, in an individual deer, when a recessive gene is paired with a dominant gene, the traits displayed by the recessive gene remain hidden. But when two deer with the recessive genes mate, the two recessive genes can get paired and become dominant.

No one knows how many deer carry the recessive trait for albinism, but in humans, about one in 200 people carry it, which only translates into about one in 20,000 humans actually becoming albinos.

Why such a difference in numbers between "normal" and albino offspring? Unless both parents carry the recessive gene, their offspring can't inherit a recessive gene. Since recessive genes for albinism are rare in the first place, the chances of two deer with the recessive gene finding each other and mating are even rarer. Even then, it's still only a one-in-four chance that the offspring they produce will be an albino. That's why mammalogists estimate that only one in 10,000 fawns will be an albino.

Confused? Here's how it works:
- A normally-colored doe with no recessive genes bred to a normally-colored buck with no recessive genes will always produce a normally-colored deer.
- Two normally-colored deer that both carry the recessive gene would have a one-in-four chance of producing an albino fawn.
- An albino doe or buck bred to a normal deer with

TWO NORMALLY-COLORED DEER THAT BOTH CARRY THE RECESSIVE GENE WOULD HAVE A ONE-IN-FOUR CHANCE OF PRODUCING AN ALBINO FAWN.

no recessive gene for albinism will always produce normally-colored fawns.

• An albino doe or buck bred to a normal deer with the recessive gene would have a one-in-two chance of producing an albino fawn.

• An albino doe bred to an albino buck will always produce albino fawns.

It's easier to see these possibilities if we use what's called a Punnett square to show the math. Since genes come in pairs, each adult deer can be represented by a pair of symbols. A capital "A" represents the dominant, or normally-colored, gene. A lower case "a" represents the recessive, or potentially albino, gene.

1.

2 deer with dominant trait

	A	A
A	AA	AA
A	AA	AA

2.

2 deer with mixed genes

	A	a
A	AA	Aa
a	Aa	aa

3.

1 mixed and 1 w/ recessive trait

	A	a
a	Aa	aa
a	Aa	aa

4.

2 deer with recessive trait

	a	a
a	aa	aa
a	aa	aa

AN ALBINO DOE BRED TO AN ALBINO BUCK WILL ALWAYS
PRODUCE ALBINO FAWNS.

In the second and third scenarios, even if the fawns produced were normally-colored, the fawns would probably still carry the recessive gene. As adults they could eventually produce an albino fawn if they mated with an albino or another deer with the recessive gene, and if the luck of the genetic draw worked out for them. ❧

Historical Accounts of White Deer

THROUGHOUT THE LAST CENTURY, THE BOULDER JUNCTION AREA IN VILAS COUNTY, WISCONSIN, HAS BEEN WELL KNOWN FOR ITS POPULATION OF WHITE DEER.

On April 24, 1950, *Life Magazine* published as its "Picture of the Week," a photo of three white deer standing among a herd of about 20 deer at Dairyman's Lodge in Boulder Junction. Sightings and stories have abounded in this area ever since settlement, and to this day, it's relatively common to see white deer.

White deer were also observed in this area as far back as the arrival of some of the first European explorers. Evidence of this comes from journals describing the complex river and portage routes that connected Lake Superior to the Wisconsin River. In 1847, Geologist J.G. Norwood described in detail the entire route to the Wisconsin River, but here I have excerpted just a few days from his journal beginning from his encampment on Trout Lake in Vilas County.

"September 30. Ice formed one-fourth of an inch thick last night. The portage between Trout and Lower Rock Lakes [Pallette and Escanaba Lakes] is about two miles and a quarter in length ... A portage of three hundred yards leads to Upper Rock Lake [Escanaba], which is one mile in its largest diameter. These lakes are also connected by a small stream. They derive their name from the immense number of boulders which line their shores, and show themselves above the water in the shallow parts ...

"We had great difficulty in finding the portage from this lake ... Three small ponds were passed in the first

two miles. They are connected by a small stream [Birch Creek] flowing into Upper Rock Lake, which is navigable for canoes up to the second pond. From this point a portage of everything has to be made to Lower White Elk Lake [White Birch Lake] …

"Lower White Elk Lake, where we camped, is about three-quarters of a mile long and a quarter of a mile wide. Here were found a number of deserted wigwams and the remains of a garden. The lake affords great numbers of fish, and the quantity of their remains scattered around shows they are the principal article of food among the Indians who occasionally inhabit it.

"October 1 … We crossed Lower White Elk Lake, and by a stream twenty feet wide and a quarter of a mile long, passed into Second White Elk Lake [Ballard Lake], which is about two miles long and one mile wide. From this we passed into Third White Elk Lake [Irving Lake], by a stream ten yards wide and three hundred yards long …

"From this lake, a portage of a quarter of a mile brought us to the Fourth White Elk Lake [Laura Lake] …

"The portage to the headwaters of the Wisconsin River starts due east from this lake."

IT'S ALSO A POSSIBILITY THAT WHITE MOOSE WERE ONCE SEEN ON THESE LAKES, AND WERE MISTAKENLY CALLED "ELK" BY THE FIRST EUROPEANS.

Norwood's description of four consecutive "White Elk Lakes" suggests that these lakes were likely named after white elk. Or, is it possible that Norwood, or whoever first named the lakes, could have mistakenly misidentified white deer as elk? If so, the naming of these lakes would indicate that a white deer population originated in this area in the 1800s, or before.

To sort out if elk and deer could have been confused isn't an easy task. Hartley Jackson writes in his book, *Mammals of Wisconsin*, "Europeans who first came to American knew about the European moose (called 'elk' in Europe) and were also familiar with the European red deer, a mammal somewhat similar to the American elk."

So, to further complicate the matter, it's also a possibility that white moose were once seen on these lakes, and were mistakenly called "elk" by the first Europeans. (It's also possible that the labeler of the lakes was three sheets to the wind and was hallucinating white elk—history is full of such non sequiturs).

However, assuming an actual connection between a true sighting of white animals and the naming of the lakes, the odds for either white elk or white moose having been seen here are extremely low. Elk and moose were found in far lower numbers in north central Wisconsin than deer. Wisconsin wildlife historian A. W. Shorger noted, "In Wisconsin, the elk was most numerous in the open woodlands, oak openings, and at the border of grassland and forest. These habitats prevailed in the southern and western parts of the state … The range of the elk in the state was strikingly like that of the buffalo, showing that the elk was also predominantly a prairie animal."

THIS SMALL SHEET OF WATER—SO CALLED, ACCORDING TO TRADITION, FROM THE CIRCUMSTANCE OF A WHITE DEER HAVING BEEN SEEN UPON ITS BANK—WAS SUPPOSED BY US TO EMPTY INTO A BRANCH OF THE WISCONSIN RIVER.

The last elk was killed in Wisconsin sometime before 1875, and while a few apparently lived in the dense woodlands of north-central Wisconsin, the mathematical likelihood of white elk living along four lakes would be exceedingly remote.

Likewise, while moose were present in northern Wisconsin, Schorger notes that moose "were most numerous in Douglas County followed by Bayfield and Burnett Counties.

The moose is notorious for shifting its range, hence it is difficult to determine from published accounts just how plentiful it was. It is certain, however, that with the exception of the caribou, it was the least numerous of the deer family."

Despite Schorger's general statement, moose must have been present at least in small numbers in the Vilas County area because as Schorger also relates, "At the post on Lac du Flambeau, Vilas County, in the winter of 1804-05, Malhiot traded for the hides, and the meat, of nine moose."

Nevertheless, the likelihood of seeing white moose on four lakes in a row is as remote as that of seeing white elk.

The best reason, however, for believing white deer were seen in this area at the time comes from the 1846 journal of A.B. Gray, just a year earlier than Norwood's. While Gray is less exacting than Norwood in his description of passing through this route, he has this to say upon leaving Trout Lake:

"The next evening we reached 'White Deer' lake with our canoes, after making several portages and passing up a small and crooked branch, with difficult swamps, through which we pushed ourselves. This small sheet of water—so

called, according to tradition, from the circumstance of a white deer having been seen upon its bank—was supposed by us to empty into a branch of the Wisconsin River."

Thus, the historic name, at least according to Gray, of at least one lake in the area is White Deer, and why Norwood called them White Elk lakes will probably remain forever unclear.

Still, "never say never" in history or biology. The sightings of white elk, white moose, or white deer are all possible explanations for the original names of these lakes. However, the remarkable coincidence of both historic and current white deer populations in this area offers the most likely explanation for the naming of these lakes. ❧

The opportunity to record moments of surprise or real survival is what keeps me in the field at every opportunity. To experience the sighting of a lynx or a young animal struggling against all odds makes me feel more alive and connected to the natural world than anything I do.

White in a World of Color — The Perils of Albinism?

MELANIN PERFORMS TWO ESSENTIAL TASKS IN MOST ANIMALS. FIRST, MELANIN IS A SUPERB NATURAL SUNSCREEN.

It protects the skin by absorbing all wavelengths of harmful ultraviolet rays of the sun, while allowing the beneficial rays for Vitamin D production to enter the body. Melanin acts in effect as the sunshine governor.

Second, melanin permits vision to fully mature by helping to develop various parts of the eyes, including irises, retinas, eye muscles, and optic nerves. The absence of melanin often results in problems with focusing, depth perception, and tracking.

For a wild animal, impaired vision can be a life and death issue. Extreme farsightedness or near-sightedness, and astigmatism are common in albino humans, as are lesser-known impairments such as *nystagmus*, an involuntary movement of the eyes back and forth, *strabismus*, when the eyes have trouble tracking together, and *photophobia*, sensitivity to light.

The question is how much do these visual impairments affect albino deer? Unfortunately, little research has been done to offer any answers. It's very likely, however, that the same visual problems that affect albino humans also affect albino deer. Poor vision would almost certainly cause deer to have trouble finding food or seeing danger.

One might also expect that a white coat would make a deer far more easily seen and eaten by predators during non-snow months (on the other hand, a white coat could provide an albino protective camouflage during the winter).

Other questions about the impact of albinism are
social: are white deer accepted within a herd structure,
and are individual albinos accepted by potential mates?

No behavioral studies exist specifically on albino deer,
but in studies of albino ravens, barn swallows, red-winged
blackbirds, and penguins, they were all consistently
rejected when trying to attract a mate. But since birds
rely far more on coloration than mammals, it may be
inappropriate to compare birds to deer. Most courting
birds rely significantly on feather colors and patterns to
identify potential mates, but for mammals, color is a
characteristic they pay much less attention to.

Several studies have tried to shed light on the
potential predation of albinos, and the results have been
mixed. One study examined whether avian predators
preferentially chose normally-colored mice or albino mice.
When captive barns owls and eastern screech owls were
released in enclosures with one brown and one white
mouse running loose, the owls more often pounced on
the albinos.

Shrikes took more albinos as well, but only when dense
cover was available, the cover presumably allowing the
brown mice to better camouflage themselves.

When the experiment was repeated with shrikes in
open areas with little cover, the mice were all easily visible,
and here the shrikes captured more brown mice.

The researchers concluded that visually-oreinted
predators use a specific hunting search image, because
when the voles were equally visible, the shrikes took the
brown voles. The odd coloring of the albinos actually
helped protect them in the open from visual hunters like
shrikes. Thus, the color of the prey appears to make little
difference as long as the prey generally looks and acts like
a known prey item.

THESE STUDIES SUGGEST THAT THE QUALITY OF A HABITAT HAS MORE TO DO WITH THE SURVIVAL OF AN ALBINO ANIMAL THAN THE COLOR OF ITS COAT.

In another study of raptors and mice, the researchers released more than 100 albino voles among a population of darker voles in a grassy enclosure with lots of cover. They found that the albino voles survived just as well as the darker voles, and actually had a better survival rate during late fall and early winter. They attributed these results to the fact that the test plot had densely matted grasses under which the voles could tunnel and hide.

The researchers then recaptured many of the albino and brown voles, and released them in a field with very sparse cover. The following year they found many brown voles, but were unable to find any albinos.

These studies suggest that the quality of a habitat has more to do with the survival of an albino animal than the color of its coat. For a white deer, this may mean that where dense cover is available in which to hide, they may be no more visible to a wolf, or a human hunter, than their tan brethren.

As for rejection by potential mates, the jury is out on white deer, but most biologists would hold that a buck in full rut, brown or albino, very likely doesn't care one iota what color the doe is.

Finally, within a herd structure, there's little evidence that white deer are particularly ostracized in any manner. In fact, the number of pictures of mixed herds of deer apparently mingling without incident suggests they generally get along fine. ✣

The first albino fawn I ever observed was bedded down among fallen white birch trees. Was it just coincidence that it was there or was it a conscious attempt by the doe to keep its offspring inconspicuous from predators? Is it possible that albino survival rate is increased simply when they frequent areas with white birch in significant amounts?

Hunting Albino Deer — Biology vs. Aesthetics

THE QUESTION OF WHETHER HUNTING ALBINO DEER SHOULD BE LEGAL RAISES THE HACKLES OF MANY HUNTERS, BUT IN DIFFERENT WAYS.

Thirteen states have made hunting albino deer illegal, including upper Midwestern states like Wisconsin, Michigan, Illinois, and Iowa. In Minnesota, however, it's legal to hunt all albino animals, except for white bears.

As with most hunting issues, there are pros and cons to hunting white deer. There's no biological value in protecting albinos, but by not hunting albinos, we increase the chances that the genetic roll of the dice will favor an albino fawn occurring. Many argue for the aesthetic benefits of seeing such rare and startling beauty as the deciding factor in the hunting debate. A few simply say it's unsporting to hunt an animal so easily seen in the wild.

Others, however, argue that recessive genetic traits, whether for albinism or any other trait, become recessive because they typically don't increase the survival potential of an animal. By encouraging more albinos in the genetic pool, some argue we are encouraging a trait that makes deer less fit for their world.

The Indiana DNR has a position paper on why they do not protect albino deer, which states, "This trait [albinism] is due to a genetic mutation and has been 'evolutionarily' selected against through history. Albino animals not only are subjected to increased predation due to the lack of adaptive camouflage, but often also have other maladaptive genetic traits … We believe that offering protection to maladapted individuals while

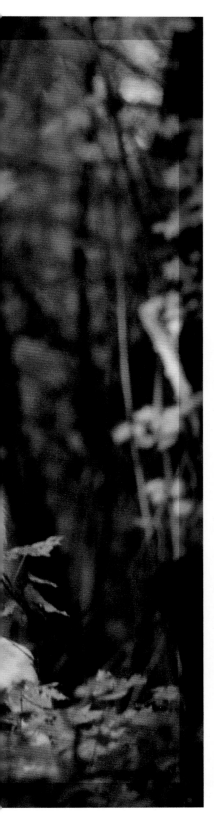

MANY ARGUE FOR THE AESTHETIC BENEFITS OF SEEING SUCH RARE AND STARTLING BEAUTY AS THE DECIDING FACTOR IN THE HUNTING DEBATE.

putting pressure on adapted individuals would not be biologically or philosophically justifiable. The novelty of seeing a 'different' animal should not overrule sound wildlife management."

If we have learned anything about deer debates, they seldom, if ever, are resolved to everyone's satisfaction. But however the debate spins in your state, no one will argue that seeing a white deer is anything less than a remarkable, if not a magical, experience. ❦

Ojibwe Story of the White Deer, Waabi Waawashkeshii

BY MINODE'I BINESHI, LAC DU FLAMBEAU ELDER

THE STORY OF WAABI WAAWASHKESHII GOES WAY BACK, ALMOST TO THE BEGINNING OF CREATION. THEY ARE HERE FOR A VERY IMPORTANT REASON.

Creator put them here—just like all plants and animals and people—for a reason. All things were meant to teach, to share, to care for one another and to be good to everyone, to live in harmony and balance.

After Creator finished the work of creation, all of *Akii*, our mother earth, was in place and living in balance and harmony. Then out of Akii, came the shape and form of iikwe, woman, who would always represent the nurturing nature of balance and harmony.

Akii became aware of the wonderment of all creation but especially noticed the beauty of *Waabanoong*, morning star. Waabanoong is the one who sets the right path for all the other sky spirits to follow. They include *giishik*, the sun, *giizis*, the moon, and *aanang*, the stars. Waabanoong also represents *biimaadizi*, the positive way of life for all beings going from east to west beginning with childhood, the east, and ending with old age, the west. Waabanoong is the first peacemaker and it is Waabanoong who first learned the mysteries and knowledge of medicinal plants.

Akii then took the shape of iikwe beginning first as *Aashkikwe*, first or new woman. Each day she noticed that just before dawn, all things became quiet and peaceful. Then the sky world slowly became light. Aashkikwe was awestruck by the beauty of this time of day and then

when Waabanoong appeared, she soon fell in love with him. When Waabanoong saw Aashkikwe looking up at him with such love and kindness, he soon came down upon Akii and as soon as he alit upon the ground, he changed into *Aashki'inini,* the first or new man. He asked Aashkikwe to be his wife but he told her that she would have to live in the sky world if she consented. He also told her there would be rules to follow in the sky world. Aashkikwe consented to be his wife, to live in the sky world and to follow all the rules of the sky world.

Waabanoong then told Aashkikwe they would live in the first level of the sky world and the spirits there would only require her to follow one rule at that level. That rule is that she could not look through the doorway of the sky, back down towards Akii. Because she is so connected to Akii, there would be no way she would be able to remain in the sky world and the sky spirits would be left with no alternative but to send her back down to Akii. She consented to the rule and promised never to look through the doorway.

From this, the Anishinabe people first began to learn that there are rules to follow in all levels of life. Without rules, life would be chaotic.

Waabanoong built *negwe*, a rainbow, and he and Aaskikwe lived there under the blessings it gave them and they lived a very good life there. But then one day when all the sky spirits were out doing their business of creation, Aashkikwe went out in the sky world to look for plant medicines. Her search slowly brought her closer and closer to the doorway of the sky world. As she drew nearer and nearer, she found some plants there that would make good food for the people so she began to dig them up. As she dug them up, she took too many of them and because she dug too deep, she made a hole in the sky

world. Out of curiosity, she looked through the hole in the sky world and down below, she saw Akii.

Just like Waabanoong had warned, Aashkikwe became very homesick for Akii. When this happened, all the sky spirits went into a great commotion and they all came there to the hole Aashkikwe had made. They told Aashkikwe they would have to send her down to Akii now because her sickness would cause great harm if they did not. They told her, as much as they loved her and as much as they could see she was going to have Waabanoong's baby, they had to follow the rule.

We do not feel anger from what Aashkikwe did. Instead today we can still learn from it. We learn not to take more than we need whether it is medicine or food. Never take more than what we will need for one season, never more. And if Aashkikwe had not returned to Aaki, today there would be no Anishinabe here. We also know that when we look in the sky, we know if snow is coming, or if rain is coming by a rainbow that will encircle the sun or the moon, two great sky spirits. We know that men are guided by the sun spirit and women are guided by the moon spirit.

So Aashkikwe was sent back to Aaki and as she fell, she screamed with fear. But the swans and geese heard her screams and they felt sorry for her so they met her half way in the sky and brought her gently back down to where she was able to step off their backs safely.

When Creator made the plants and animals, he gave them all a purpose. Each would live their lives according

MOKWA, BEAR, GAVE HIS LIFE TO SAVE AASHKI'ININI, FIRST MAN. WAAWASHKESHI, DEER, GAVE HIS LIFE TO SAVE AASHKIKWE, FIRST WOMAN. MOKWA IS THE PROTECTOR AND GUARDIAN, WAAWASHKESHI IS THE GENTLE AND KIND SPIRIT.

to rules set for each of them. By living this way, they would help each other. Some of them were medicine and some were food. Others were teachers. It is said that each one shall live its life according to Creators' intention. By doing so, all life would be in harmony. When one gives his life to another, it is because the other needs food, or a certain medicine, or a teaching. In that way, the one who gave his life, fulfills his purpose in the name of Creator.

Today, if we followed that purpose, if we cared for all the plants, the animals, the waters, the sky and most importantly, Akii, we would be much better off. If we cared for the waters, when a fish takes in that water from one place, and a food from another place, and mixes it together in a mystery way, that fish makes medicine for you, perhaps not for me, but for you. If you live your life in harmony, you might receive that medicine from that fish. And so we conduct our lives in a ceremonial way, respecting all living things, living in harmony with them.

Many of the animals received certain powers from Creator. Different ones gave their lives first to the Anishinabe so that Anishinabe would be safe, strong and healthy. *Mokwa*, bear, gave his life to save aashki'inini, first man. *Waawashkeshi*, deer, gave his life to save Aashkikwe, first woman. Mokwa is the protector and guardian, Waawashkeshi is the gentle and kind spirit.

It was *Eyaabe*, a buck deer, who gave his life to Aashkikwe to feed her and to give her warmth from his hide that she would tan and make into clothing. From this first food, Anishinabe has learned the

AND SO IT IS WITH ALL ANIMALS, THEY ALL HAVE THEIR LEADERS
AND AS WELL, THEY ALSO HAVE THEIR WHITE ONES WHO REPRESENT
THEIR SPECIAL KIND OF SPIRITUALITY.

gift of kindness, of peace and of sharing. The flesh of waawashkeshi should always be shared with others in need and especially with elders. When a hunter kills his first waawashkeshi, a feast should always be held, not so much to celebrate the young hunter's feat but to honor the life of waawashkeshi. But it also serves notice to others that the young hunter has now taken on a new responsibility to all the people as a provider.

Among all the waawashkeshi, there are several leaders, the male buck being one of them and then the white buck who is known as waabi waawashkeshi. This white one represents the sacredness of all living things and they should be left alone, never hunted or bothered. When we see them, we should take notice of our own spirituality and think about where we are with it. Are we taking care of it or are we neglecting it? Anishinabe will put *asema*, tobacco offerings, down by a rock, or in the water, or by a tree, or in the fire, and they will talk about waabi waawashkeshi and ask for direction with their own spirituality.

And so it is with all animals, they all have their leaders and as well, they also have their white ones who represent their special kind of spirituality. From this, we will know that each of us have our own special kind of spirituality; and though it may not be like others, that is okay, because strength comes from each one. ❧

A white moon peers through twilight clouds
over a still lake dimpled by frog song.
Above, a young white deer peers into the golden
mozaic of woods, all senses attuned.

Few things give me as much joy as exploring a winding woods road—the unknown, the curious, the seldom-seen appearing perhaps around the next bend.

I know my life has been enriched in ways only nature can, touched to the core by the white deer—ghost deer—spirit deer.

The unique and unusual enrich our lives
and contribute to the complexity of nature.
Biodiversity is the immune system of the natural
world. Impair it and you destroy the planet's
ability to survive change.